D1259546

For Morgan.
—C.D.
For Colin and Veda.
—P.D.

Text © 2022 Corinne Demas
Illustrations © 2022 Penelope Dullaghan

Book design by Melissa Nelson Greenberg

Published in 2022 by CAMERON + COMPANY, a division of ABRAMS.
All rights reserved. No portion of this book may be reproduced,
stored in a retrieval system, or transmitted in any form or by any means,
mechanical, electronic, photocopying, recording, or otherwise,
without written permission from the publisher.

Library of Congress Cataloging-in-Publication Data available.
ISBN: 978-1-951836-42-9

Printed in China

10 9 8 7 6 5 4 3 2 1

CAMERON KIDS is an imprint of CAMERON + COMPANY

CAMERON + COMPANY
Petaluma, California
www.cameronbooks.com

The Perfect Tree

words by Corinne Demas

pictures by Penelope Dullaghan

cameron kids

On the day before Christmas, Bunny made a string of red berries and cut out a shiny star.

Then she put on her muffler and mittens and set out to find the perfect Christmas tree, one that was just her size.

Squirrel was collecting pine cones in the woods. "Where are you off to this morning?" he asked.

"I'm looking for the perfect Christmas tree," said Bunny.

"A perfect tree should be bushy," said Squirrel,
"just like my tail. Try looking in the meadow."

So Bunny went off to the meadow to look for the perfect tree. She found a tree that was just her size, but it wasn't bushy like Squirrel's tail.

Mole heard Bunny passing by and poked her nose out of her hole. "What are you looking for?" asked Mole.

"I'm looking for the perfect Christmas tree," said Bunny.

"A perfect tree should have a point on the top for a star, just like my nose," said Mole. "I don't get out much, but I believe you'll find one in the far field."

So Bunny climbed over the stone wall and looked in the
far field for the perfect tree.

She found a tree that was just her size and bushy like
Squirrel's tail, but it didn't have a point on top for a star.

Cardinal was perched on a branch nearby.
"What are you looking for?" asked Cardinal.

"I'm looking for the perfect Christmas tree," said Bunny.

"It's color that counts!" cried Cardinal. "A perfect tree should be the greenest green. Look down by the stream."

So Bunny looked down by the stream. She found a tree that was just her size. It was as bushy as Squirrel's tail, and it had a point on top for a star. But it wasn't the greenest green.

Skunk stuck her head out of a hollow log.
"What are you looking for?" she asked.

"I'm looking for the perfect Christmas tree," said Bunny.

"It's the smell that matters," Skunk said. "A perfect tree should smell like Christmas. You might look up the mountain."

So Bunny climbed up the mountain. She sat down on a rock to catch her breath before she started searching again.

There were so many trees!

Bunny found a tree that was almost perfect. It was just her size. It was as bushy as Squirrel's tail. It was the greenest green. It had a point on top for a star. But it didn't smell like Christmas.

Deer came wandering out of the thicket.
"What are you looking for?" asked Deer.

"I'm looking for the perfect Christmas tree," said Bunny.

"What makes it perfect?" asked Deer.

"It should be just my size. It should be bushy. It should have a point on top for a star. It should be the greenest green. And it should smell like Christmas," said Bunny.

"Did you look in the meadow?" asked Deer.

"Yes," said Bunny.

"Did you look in the far field?"

"Yes," said Bunny. "And I looked along the river. And I looked all over the mountain."

"Maybe there isn't a perfect tree," said Deer.

"Or maybe I just haven't found it yet," said Bunny.

But it was getting cold, and Bunny couldn't look any longer.
It was time to head home.

She climbed down the mountain and hiked along the stream,
across the far field, over the stone wall,
through the meadow, and into the woods.

Bunny was close to home when she saw a tree she hadn't noticed before.
It was just her size and as bushy as Squirrel's tail.
It had a point on top for a star.
It was the greenest green.
And when she got close, it smelled like Christmas.

The perfect tree.

Bunny ran into her house and got her saw.
She hurried back to cut her perfect Christmas tree.

But the tree looked so perfect, right where it was, Bunny couldn't
bear to cut it down.

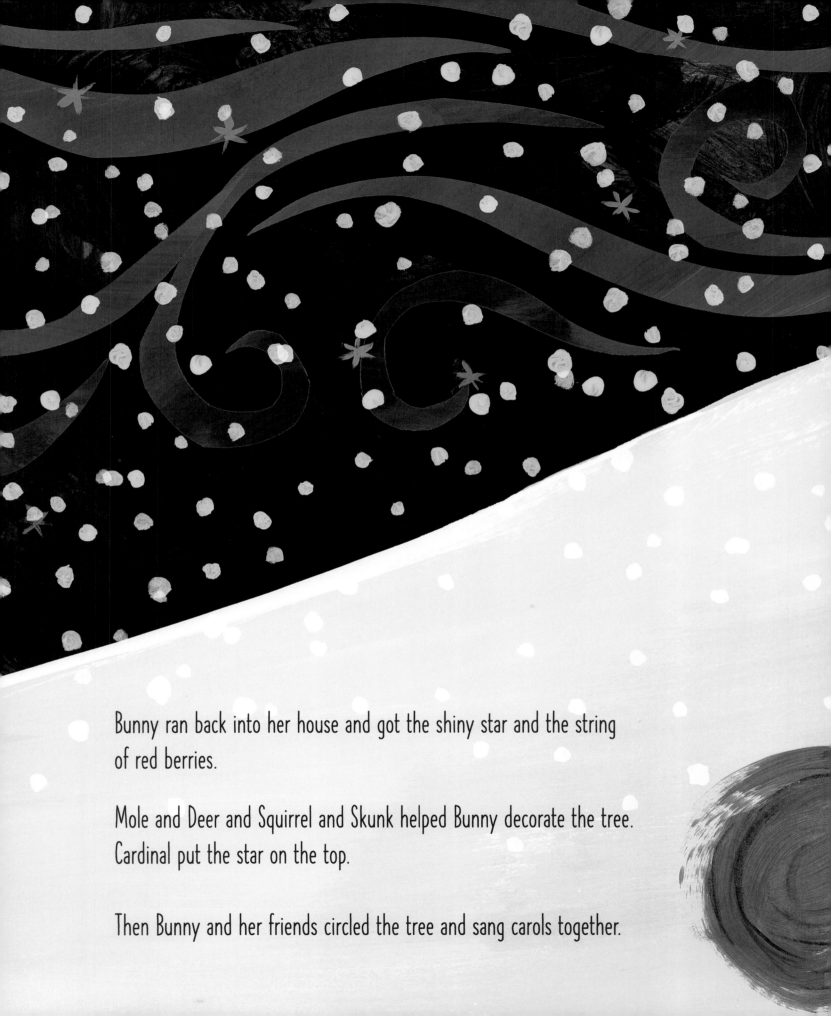

Bunny ran back into her house and got the shiny star and the string of red berries.

Mole and Deer and Squirrel and Skunk helped Bunny decorate the tree. Cardinal put the star on the top.

Then Bunny and her friends circled the tree and sang carols together.

And now it really was the perfect Christmas tree.